Orla was Six

Orla Was Six

Mary Beckett

Children's
POOLBEG

28201

Contents

A Pig in a Boat

A Pig in a Boat

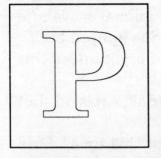iers was a pig. He lived in a boat. You could not sail in the boat. You could not row the boat. It was an old boat turned upside down on a grassy place in the rocks at Cushendun. Piers lived in under it. There were cracks between the old timbers of the boat. They let in the light and air. A square of wood was cut away and covered with wire, fastened with loops over nails so that Piers could be fed. It was through that square that he looked out at the sea.

It was through that square that he saw the children every day in July. They stayed in a house along the path. They had to pass by his boat to get to the sand.

There were two boys and a little girl of six called Orla. It was Orla who discovered that there was a pig under the boat. She leaned against it to shake the sand out of her shoes. She felt the animal move and she heard him snuffle. She jumped back.

"Hugh, Hugh! There's a pig under this boat."

"Do you hear silly Orla!" Art said, but they came back.

"Art, I'm not silly. Not this time," Orla said and they looked in through the wire square.

"We'll heave up the boat and let him out," Orla said, but Hugh, the bigger boy said, "No. We can't do that. He might bite your leg off. Pigs are very dangerous, you know."

Piers did not know. He didn't think he would bite Orla's pink legs, but he didn't know what pigs did generally. He had been alone under this boat since he left his mother's warm, smelly side and his squealing, nipping brothers and sisters. They did nip. They all did. So did he.

Maybe they would all bite when they grew bigger.

"Hello Pig!" Art shouted in and Piers snorted back.

"He needs a name," Orla said. "We can't call him Pig."

Hugh and Art often helped her with names for her dolls.

"Call him Peter," Art said. "He is in a boat and Peter means a rock, and he lives like a rock in there."

"These rocks are black and he's pink," Hugh said. "Anyway, Peter is a saint's name. You can't call a pig a saint's name."

"Call him Porky," Orla said, but they both shouted "Oh no," and rolled their eyes at how silly she was, so she kept quiet.

"What about Piers?" Hugh said. "It is the same name as Peter. There is a book called Piers Plowman I've heard of."

"Hello Piers," Art said. "Do you like to be called Piers?"

Orla thought she would call him Piers too, because she liked to agree, but to her a pier meant the road at the far side of the beach where the two hotels were. It was beside the river, so they had been told not to let Orla go over there. In the sea beyond the mouth of the river there were nets, and men stood up in boats doing something about salmon.

"Mammy is calling," Art said. "Dinner is ready," and they ran off towards their house.

Piers liked his new name. The stout man and his stout wife, who owned him and fed him, never called him anything. They put his bucket of food in on a rope and pulled it out empty the next day. They gave him plenty to eat. They did not mean to be unkind.

The next day, the children came again, this time with two dogs. The dogs sniffed around the boat and the brown spaniel barked a bit. "Teddy, keep quiet," Art said and Teddy went off across the rocks.

"Bran is a good dog," Orla said, patting the other one and his black tail thumped against the boat. Then there was a fuss because Teddy slid off a steep slanty rock into the sea. He could swim well, but he could not scramble back up the rock, so the two boys ran over to pull him up. Orla stayed beside the boat because she did not like the deep parts of the sea.

"Piers, do you like the sea?" she asked the pig. "Teddy is a very silly dog, Daddy says. Bran is sensible and well-behaved, but Teddy has never learnt sense. He's not a pup any longer, you know."

Teddy ran back to the path, shaking himself so that the drips of sea water flew around every place, even into Piers's boat. He licked them off his snout.

Hugh and Art were pushing each other about, laughing. Their clothes were all wet. "We can lick off all the sea water," they said and pretended to enjoy it.

"Mmm."

"We can dry ourselves when Mammy brings the towels," Hugh said. They could not go in to swim until she came. She had told them to go ahead, that she was still struggling with the Aga. They had an electric cooker at home in Belfast.

When they were gone Piers licked again at the drops of sea-water and told himself they were a good taste, but he was used to salt caked on his face from the sea air that blew in the wire square that was his window. By the end of each day it flavoured the bucket of scraps that fed him.

Every morning, Orla talked to Piers. She told him to admire the blue of the sea, or the white tops on the waves, or the spray at the rocks. The two boys ran on with their dogs and then had to wait for her.

"Oh come on, Orla," they shouted. "Mammy says you are beginning to smell of pig."

"I don't care," Orla said. "I think Piers has a nice smell." They jumped up and down and shouted "Pooh" at her.

One damp dull day while Orla was telling Piers how lucky he was to be sheltered under his boat, a man came along. He was a tall man in a long raincoat, old enough to be a grandfather. He stood there looking at Orla.

"There is a pig in there," Orla told him. Her brothers hearing her different voice, came back with the dogs. Hugh took one of her hands and Art took the other, because they knew that it might not be safe to talk to a stranger. Orla had forgotten that. With two big brothers and two dogs to protect her she would be safe, since they were within sight of the house.

"Hello, young man, what's your name?" the man said to Hugh who arrived first.

"I'm Hugh O'Neill," he said and the man laughed.

"And you?"

"I'm Art O'Neill."

"I'm Orla O'Neill, 24 Kelvin Drive Belfast, and my phone number is 745284," Orla said. She had been taught that for fear she was ever lost.

"Belfast!" the man said "A wretched place."

Orla thought he meant "a wrecked place" so she said "Bits of it get wrecked, but it gets fixed up again very soon."

"Wretched! Wretched! A wretched place! That's what I said. I never go there."

"It's not bad," Hugh put in. "It's all right to live in and to go to school in." Hugh was in a school for big boys and he liked it.

"What's your name?" Orla asked.

"My name? Lord of the Glens, would that do?"

"You're English," Orla said, because of the way he spoke. Hugh shook her arm to make her keep quiet. She did not understand that big people often do not like questions about themselves.

"What's this about a pig?" he asked, walking right round the boat. There wasn't a sound out of Piers. "Is this children's nonsense?"

"No. No," they all shouted. "Look in the wire square." He did, stooping down.

"Good Lord, you're right," he said. "Something will have to be done about this. Who owns it?" They pointed to a battered cottage behind a wall.

"Would the pig like to live in a field?" the

man said to them. "What would you think?
Are you friends of his?"

Orla told him that he was a great friend
and that he might love a field, but she
would miss him.

"You could come and visit him," he said,
but Hugh nudged her to stop her saying
yes.

"When I was at Oxford long ago, I saw
pigs in fields with little huts for shelter
during bad weather," he told them and
then he went off, back across the rocks and
around the beach.

"He's not a lord, he's a loonie," Hugh said
and they laughed and kept on repeating
the words because they sounded so well.

Then Art said in an imitation English
accent "Good Lord, you're right!" and they
had a great time at that.

The next morning, he was beside the
boat with a big old car and a wooden truck
behind. In the truck stood Piers, blinking
and snorting. The boys hung back but Orla
ran up to the truck.

"Oh Piers, you are out in the sunshine.

Isn't it lovely and warm." Then she turned to the tall man. "How did you get him into the truck? Did you lift him in?"

"His owner whacked him in," the man said, nodding over towards the cottage. The boat was the same as ever.

"Wouldn't you think they would turn it over to air it?" Art said.

"We did not discuss it," the man said. "I told him it was against the law to keep a pig in such conditions. I bought it from him. It will have a field instead of a boat."

"Good-bye, Piers," Orla said.

"Come and visit him, Moira," he said and the boys tittered, but he did not notice. He took out paper and a biro. "See, I'll draw a map to show you how to reach the field." He traced out the roads and paths from the boat to the fields, showing it all to Hugh and Art. Orla was too young to understand it. He started the car and the truck bounced up and down on the bumpity path. Orla wondered how you would know if a pig looked happy. She gazed after his unsteady head.

Hugh was studying the little map. "It is away from the sea," he said.

"We could walk there easily enough, but we had better not go on our own. It's well it's Friday. Daddy will be here this evening." Their father worked all week in Belfast and came to Cushendun at weekends. He agreed to bring them on Saturday morning to see Piers.

It was not very far, but the roads were new to them and their father walked very fast. They dropped behind several times and had to run, holding Orla by the hand, to catch up with him. Orla's legs were tired when they reached the field marked X on the map.

Hugh and Art stood up on the stout bars of the gate and Orla was lifted in her father's arms, although she felt she was too old for that. It was a nice, grassy field, not very big. It had hedges all round and a hut in the middle.

"It's a good field for a pig," Orla said. "Isn't it, Daddy? But I can't see him. Piers!" she called. "Piers, where are you?"

And out of the hut came his head and front trotters. He snorted and began to run towards the gate, but he stumbled and fell down on his knees. Orla knew just how he felt, but Art was worried.

"What's the matter with him?" he asked.

"I suppose his legs were not used much under that boat," Hugh said.

"He's not in training," his father laughed, but they did not think it funny to see poor Piers so feeble. He got to the gate at last and Orla had to be kept from hugging him, as he shoved his head against the bars.

"Your legs will soon grow strong," she told him, "out in the nice fresh air."

"We'll come back next Saturday," Daddy said. "He'll exercise them all week. Pigs are very clever animals you know. By next Saturday he'll be in clover," and he laughed again.

"But he is in clover now," Orla said. "The field is full of clover."

"Daddy is making a joke," Hugh said. "Being in clover means having everything to suit you." He didn't think much of his father's jokes.

"Can we not come back before that?" Orla asked. "He'll be lonely."

"Get your mother to bring you," Daddy said and they all knew that was no good. Mammy did not like walks.

For the last week of their holidays, the sun shone. They spent most of it on the beach, digging forts in the sand, swimming, and flinging themselves down on the rug beside Mammy. She could now work the Aga well, and so had time to come out and enjoy her holiday. They rarely gave Piers a thought. Sometimes Orla did for a moment in bed, and then she fell asleep.

In the field, Piers loved the sun too, but every morning when he woke up he had to blink and blink until he was used to it. He looked every day for the bucket of scraps and was upset for a time until his nose led him to the trough of fresh food. A man filled it every day. He came into the field, fixed up the food, said "There you go" and went off again. Nobody else came near Piers. His legs grew strong and sometimes he rolled in the grass with delight, so that his skin was pink and clean.

"Oh look, Daddy, doesn't he look well!" Orla said and he came trotting over to the gate. "Piers, you are a lovely pig. You really are a lovely pig."

Daddy sat down on the bank at the side of the road. The two dogs sniffed round the gate post and then Bran flung himself down in the grass beside Daddy, while Teddy tore across an empty field looking for rabbits.

"Were you lonely without me," Orla asked. "The sea was beautiful all week, blue and warm for swimming. We had to keep Mammy company on the beach. And we are going home to Belfast tomorrow night. Our holiday is over. You'll be all right here, won't you Piers? You won't miss us and you won't miss the sea?"

"Come on back to the beach. Your mother will think you are lost," Daddy said. The two boys started a race and Orla took her father's hand.

Piers stood at the gate, his snout between the bars. He got the faint whiff of the sea from the children and from the dogs. He would miss that. He would miss Orla and Art and Hugh. However, he had heard that pigs are very clever animals. He knew that nothing is ever quite perfect in this world.

Goldfish in a Bowl

Goldfish in a Bowl

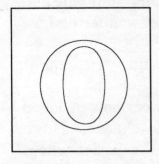ne Saturday, Art went to a fair in Hugh's school and brought home a goldfish. It looked beautiful. It swam in a plastic bag of water and it was bright gold, brighter than Mammy's rings, the brightest gold Orla had ever seen.

"Where did you get that?" Mammy asked.

"I won it," Art said, holding it up carefully. "It was the prize for throwing rings onto hooks. Hugh didn't win anything."

"Isn't it beautiful!" Orla said. "Isn't it just beautiful!"

"Oh it is, indeed," Mammy said. "But where will it live? It can't stay in a plastic

21

bag. And what will it eat? I know nothing about goldfish."

"Are you sorry I won it?" Art asked.

"Oh, not at all, Art. I am glad you had such a good aim. I am just wondering how to look after it properly."

"Ask Daddy," Orla said. "He might know."

"He's always talking about how he loved fishing when he got the chance," Hugh said. So Orla went out to the garden where Daddy was leaning on his spade talking to the man next door.

"Daddy, you have to go and buy a bowl," Orla said loudly. She was afraid the shop would be shut if she waited politely for a chance to speak. "Art won a goldfish and it is in a plastic bag, but it needs a goldfish bowl and some food."

"I'd better see what all this is about," Daddy said and the two men gave a bit of a laugh. He stepped out of his rubber boots on the mat outside the back door and put on his shoes. He agreed that the goldfish was beautiful and when Mammy told him how clever Art had been, he said "Oh, indeed yes. A great boy."

Art and Orla were going with Daddy in the car, but Hugh said he would stay at home. Orla felt that he was a bit cross. "Won't you mind the fish?" she said, but he said nothing and Mammy told her to hurry up or Daddy might go without her. They sat in the back seat, driving round quite a bit to find parking for the car and then had to walk through several streets to the pet shop.

It was a small shop—very narrow. A fat man stood looking into a fish tank so that he blocked the way in.

"Let the children pass," the man behind the counter shouted and they squeezed in past the fat man and past a row of bird cages, carefully, so as not to knock down things. Orla did not like the heavy smell of all the pet food, but she said nothing about that.

"This lad won a goldfish," Daddy said at the counter. "We need a bowl for one fish."

"Maybe we should get another fish," Orla

said. "Maybe Art's fish would be lonely. Could we buy another fish Daddy? Couldn't we?"

"Of course you could," the shopkeeper said. "You are a very sensible wee girl. A fish in a bowl on his own would be very lonely. They're not dear," he added to their father. So they walked back to the car holding a glass bowl filled with water and another goldfish swimming round and round, his eyes popping out of his head. They also had four packets of fish food, because Daddy said he did not want to have to go back to that shop too often.

The two fish were the same size, but the one from the shop was not such a pretty gold. There were little green tips on his fins. Orla watched to see would they like each other but they took no notice. They swam and swam, round and round.

"What will we call them?" Orla asked, but Hugh said "Fish don't get names." Art shook in a little of the beady food as the man in the pet shop had told him to do. They came up to the top of the water with their mouths open to gobble it.

"They're hungry," Hugh said. "You're starving them." He poured in a tablespoon of the food and some of it sank to the bottom and some floated on top, and the water turned cloudy so that the fish did not look so bright and beautiful.

The next morning, there was a heavy, nasty smell from the bowl. Before the children went to school Daddy had to change the water, although he was in a hurry to go to work. He was not pleased, but he was very handy, so he was able to do it quickly. When Orla came home from school, she saw that the bowl was gone from the top of the fridge in the kitchen. Her mother said she had to put it into the dining-room which they used only when they had visitors and for the piano.

"There is still a smell, Orla," Mammy said. "I don't like it where the food is."

"But you like the fish, don't you Mammy?" Orla asked.

"Yes, of course," Mammy said, but Orla wondered did she mean it. She went into the dining-room and stood in front of the fireplace watching the goldfish. The bowl was a bit wide for the mantelpiece.

"I tried putting them on the piano," Mammy called in from the kitchen, "but I was afraid they would die of fright when you began to play it." Orla laughed and sat down on the piano-stool. She played last month's piece of music, which she knew well, and she kept her eye on the goldfish to see how they liked it. They just swam.

Granny came to visit. She lived in Dublin and when she came to Belfast she stayed for a few days. She slept in Orla's room and Orla slept on a camp bed in the dining-room. She loved Granny's visits. Granny hugged her and told her she was a lovely girl and admired her clothes and bought her new dresses. She always brought Bewley's coffee that smelt so nice when Daddy and Mammy and Granny had it after dinner. Granny was fond of all three children, but Orla felt she was especially fond of her, because she was her only grand-daughter. Orla showed her the fish and she said "They are very pretty, but I don't think I could grow attached to them. Do you?"

That night, Mammy tucked her into the camp bed as well as possible. Camp beds are not easy to tuck. They said night prayers and Orla settled down to go to sleep. Hugh and Art were doing their homework in their bedroom. She could hear the quiet talk of the grown-ups in the sitting-room. It gave her a comfortable feeling and her eyes began to close. Then she heard the goldfish giving little gasps. "Pop. Pop. Pop," they said over and over again. Orla imagined their mouths up out of the water. "Pop. Pop. Pop." there was no end to it. They did not seem to go to sleep. After what Orla thought was a long, long time she could stand it no longer. She got up and went into the sitting-room. "Mammy," she began, but Granny said "Surely Orla is not being silly about going to bed. I always thought Orla was a good girl." Orla nearly cried.

"What is it, love?" Mammy asked.

"It's the goldfish, Mammy," Orla said very politely. "Could you please take them out for the night. They are gasping."

"Gasping!" Granny said, smiling, but Mammy said "I know what you mean, love. I'll take out the bowl."

Next morning at breakfast, Orla asked "Does Granny know I'm still a good girl? She doesn't think I'm a nuisance?"

"Of course she knows you're always a good girl," Mammy said. Granny got her breakfast in bed on a tray.

"It's Art's fault," Hugh said. "He doesn't look after his stupid fish."

"They live in there," Art said. "How was I to know they would keep Orla awake!"

"Everybody knows you can't sleep in the same room as fish. They give out poison gas at night," Hugh said and got up from the table.

"Oh, will you stop talking nonsense," Mammy said, but he was gone off laughing to wash his teeth.

At newstime in Orla's bright, cheerful school at the top of the hill, she told about the fish gasping. She imitated the look and sound of the fishes' mouths and the teacher laughed and made her do it over again. So she was in good form when she came home to keep Granny company while Mammy went out to do the messages.

When Daddy went away because of his work, Mammy had to change the water in the bowl. She did not like to do it. She said she was not handy like Daddy, but Orla knew she was good at all the important things. It was not important to be able to hammer nails or empty fish bowls. But one day as she watched Mammy empty the water, the fish slipped out into the sink and Mammy said "Mercy," and tried to grab them, but they slid out of her hand.

"Put your hand over the plug hole," she told Orla. She did that, and felt the fishy bodies against the side of her thumb. "Oh, merciful hour!" Mammy said, the way Granny did, but between them they got the two fish safely back into clean water. Then Mammy hugged Orla and said, "Well, I don't know about you, Orla, but I'll never

get fond of those fish. Only don't tell Art I
said so."

That night, even though she was back in
her own comfortable bed, in her own room,
Orla had a terrible dream. She dreamed
the fish slipped out of the water but she
had to catch them all by herself. Mammy
stood, doing nothing. When she touched
the slimy bodies, the two fish grew wings
and flew up on the white tiles beside the
cooker. She stood on a stool in her dream
and snatched at one and a gauzy wing
came off in her hand and she fell off the
stool, shouting. She wakened up on her
bedroom floor with Mammy opening the
door and turning on the lamp.

"Oh, Mammy, I had a terrible dream
about those fish," she said, holding on to
Mammy's hands to stop her going away.

"Did you love? Tell me about it in the
morning. Are you right awake now? I'll get
you a glass of water and leave your lamp
lit." Mammy was in her bare feet, half
asleep.

Orla heard Daddy mumble from the bed

"What's wrong? What's up?" and Mammy said, "Something will have to be done about those goldfish. They have Orla in a state and Hugh and Art bicker in a way they never did. They used to be good friends."

But the goldfish were still in their bowl in the dining-room in the first really cold morning of the winter.

"Were the fish cold last night, I wonder," Orla said, and Daddy answered "Oh, yes, indeed they were. Ice all over the water and the poor fish with their heads stuck up through, to gasp for breath."

"What did you do?" Orla asked although she knew it was not true.

"Your Mammy took a kettle of boiling water and poured it over them. It was a bit hot for them, but it melted the ice. Lucky it didn't crack the bowl. We'd have had a flood in the dining-room." Orla squealed and Mammy said "Oh, Conn, stop it, will you. You're worse than the boys."

"What did we do?" they asked in one voice and everybody laughed.

Orla went in after breakfast to make sure Daddy had made up all of that and when she came home from school, she looked again. She called "Mammy, Mammy, come in here. There's something wrong with one of the fish." Mammy was putting away the messages she'd bought while meeting Orla outside her school, but she came in at once. The fish was floating on his back at the top of the water. He was dead. They could both see that.

"Oh dear," Mammy said. "We can't leave him there with the other poor fish. We can't even leave him until Daddy comes home." Then she had an idea. "I know," she said. "You take your spade that you had at the seaside and dig a hole beside a rose bush." Orla did that although the ground was hard to dig. Then Mammy took a ladle and lifted out the dead fish and some water and carried him out and put him in the hole and buried him. She found an old ice-pop stick an gave it to Orla to stick it in the ground to mark the spot.

Later when Art came home from school,

Orla ran to tell him, but he did not care a bit. "Fish are no good," he said to Mammy. "I don't even like them anymore." And he sat down beside Bran on the sofa and put his head on Bran's head and Bran thumped his tail.

"Do you know what I'll do?" Mammy asked. She put on her coat and lifted the bowl. "I'll go round to Mrs. Blair. She has a pond in her back garden and she said the fish could live there if Art said so. I'll be only a minute. Will you two be safe on your own?" She was back in two minutes with the empty bowl.

"We're all happy now," Daddy said when they told him, but Orla said "Could a cat get him? Is he safe?"

"He'll just have to take his chance like the rest of us," Daddy said. Then he went on. "I meant to tell you that I was talking the other day to a man from Cushendun. He was telling me that the pig you met in the summer has two other pigs in the field for company and two other sheds for shelter. Your friend is happy with his peers." He laughed and Hugh smiled at the joke. Orla did not know if she should believe it, but she liked to imagine it was true.

Birds in the Garden

Birds in the Garden

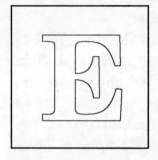

very morning before school, Orla fed the birds. When she was a little fat three-year-old girl she held the plate of crumbs in front of her tummy and called "Come on birds. Here's your breakfast." The sparrows came at once, nearly tripping her.

Now she was six. She helped Mammy clear the breakfast table. She scraped all the crumbs on one plate. Then she looked in the bread bin to see if there was any stale bread. Mammy told her what to use. If the end slice of the pan loaf was left she put it out whole so that the birds could peck at it all day. She put the crumbs in the middle of the grass, well away from the bushes. She knew that cats hid in the bushes, waiting to pounce on birds. She did that every day. Her grandfather had told her that house-sparrows cannot live without people to feed them.

The blackbirds were awake first. Before the sun rose on Winter mornings Orla could see the blackbirds hopping in the dark garden. They did not like bread much. After rain they pulled up worms like elastic bands. They ate apples. They pecked at them until the skin was empty and collapsed. There were five blackbirds in Orla's garden and they bickered and fought. Orla often had to go out for fear they would hurt one another.

They fought about their bath. They loved their bath. It was an upside down lid from an old bin. Orla's Daddy kept it full of water and mended the holes that let the water leak. On even the coldest days the blackbirds fought about whose turn it was in the water. They splashed with their wings, but no bird could splash like the starlings.

The starlings were messy birds. Scraps of food flew everywhere from their beaks. If food was left in Bran's dish or Teddy's dish the starlings stood in there and made such a mess that only a very hungry dog would touch it after them. The food was scattered in little specks on the path all round the dishes. They did not come every day. Sometimes they were away for weeks. Sometimes they arrived in flocks, pecking away all over the grass. They built their nest in the gutters or under the eaves. So did the sparrows. They had an enemy—the magpie.

"Why are they so horrible?" Orla asked her Daddy. They were beautiful birds with their white plump breasts and shiny black tilting tails. But they attacked baby birds in their nests. Orla was wakened in the early morning in Spring with the birds in a state over her window. Then she heard the clack-ack-ack-ack-ack of the magpie. She knocked the window but it took no notice. She had to waken Daddy.

"Get up, Daddy. Get up. The magpie is at

the nest over my window." Daddy came in, opened the window wide, clapped his hands and shouted until the magpie flew away.

"Some day I'll shoot those magpies," Daddy said, but of course he would not. He had no gun. Orla had to lie awake for fear the magpie came back. He often did. Sometimes Daddy would not waken again and Mammy had to come.

The sparrows were no bother. They came in the morning, calling to one another, and ate what they wanted. During the day, if a dark cloud came, they rushed to eat again.

"Why do they do that, Mammy?" she asked but nobody could tell her. Orla liked to see bread left for fear they did need it later on but the pigeons liked to clear away every crumb. The big fat wood pigeons could hardly walk on their flat pink feet. They tweaked at the food so that it flew up in the air. Sometimes, bread landed on their backs and they went around looking for it. Once, a pigeon ate

through a slice of bread and got the crust
hung round its neck like a picture frame.
Mammy laughed, watching it from the
kitchen window, but Orla ran out to help
it. It flapped away and the crust dropped
off. Sometimes a whole flock of town
pigeons came down from the roof like an
avalanche but Mammy always chased
them. She called them "gurrier" pigeons
but that was a Dublin word. Nobody in
Belfast knew about gurriers.

"We don't get any strange birds," Orla
said, when she looked through a bird book.
"Maybe if we put out proper food for them
they would come. The radio said to make a
cake of nuts and fat."

"I have no time," Mammy said. "They
will just have to do with bread." She put
out cheese at times, and the crows came
and nearly murdered one another over it.
They also fought over pastry dough that
Mammy said was too long in the fridge.

Swans flew over, necks stretched, their
big heavy wings beating at the air. On bad
Winter days seagulls wheeled overhead

but they never came down into the garden, although they came into the school yard after lunchtime. When it snowed Orla put on her rubber boots and put bread and fat on an old black-board of hers so that it would not sink in the snow. That was not a good idea. The birds teetered and slid on the shiny board.

One afternoon, Mammy and Orla came home from school and Orla went upstairs to her room. She heard a sound from the boy's bedroom. She ran down.

"Mammy, there's something in Hugh's room," she said.

"What do you mean?" Mammy asked.

"There's a noise," Orla said.

"Did you look in?" Mammy asked, taking her hand.

"I could see nothing," Orla said. "But I heard it." They stood listening in the hall. All was quiet.

"There you are," Mammy said "Not a thing." Then the scuffling noise began again.

"Is it a mouse?" Mammy asked and Orla

said "Oh no," because Mammy did not like mice. If she saw one in the yard or under the press she called Bran and he had to run barking to chase it.

"We'll go up and see what it is," Mammy said and they went upstairs, hand in hand.

In the boys' room the noise came from behind the book shelves. There had been a fire place, but to make more space Daddy had taken it away and covered the gap with hardboard.

"It's a bird in the chimney," Mammy said and Orla wondered what they would do.

"We'll shift the bookshelves to let it out. It may fly around. The door will have to be shut and the window open. Do you want to help or would you rather go out?"

"I'll help," Orla said and she shut the door behind her.

"A crow came down the chimney in Ryan's sitting-room," Mammy said. "It flew round the room leaving soot all over the walls. They had new paint, too. It was a mess."

"I hope this one won't spoil Hugh's bed or Art's," Orla said. Mammy was kneeling down in front of the books.

"Come on Orla," she said. "help me with these."

The bird in behind was banging his wings against the board. Orla hurried. She did not even look through the boys' books although she was tempted. She loved looking at their books but they complained if she moved them. Hugh had two shelves. So had Art. When half the books were in stacks on the floor Mammy thought she could shift the shelves. She checked that the curtains were well back, and the window wide open and the blind up. Then she told Orla to stand away and lifted the shelves far enough for the bird to fly out. There was a slight hollow below the board and Mammy said.

"Orla, look at its pale little bill sticking out." Then a small dark head with a bright eye appeared, sideways.

"That's no crow," Mammy said "it's a starling."

Then there was a flurry and the bird squeezed underneath and flew straight through the open window.

"Oh, wasn't that well done," Mammy said, pleased. She stayed to tidy the room. Orla went out to play.

When Daddy came home she began to tell him.

"Did you know, Daddy, when we came home from school to-day we heard something upstairs?"

"What are you talking about?" Daddy said, reading the paper.

"We heard a noise in the boys' bedroom and we crept upstairs," Orla told him, standing beside him so that he would listen. He put down the paper.

"Is this true, Anne?" he asked Mammy. "You heard someone and you crept upstairs? You surely did not!"

"We heard something, not someone," Orla said but they were talking to each other. Daddy had put away the paper and was standing with his hands on Mammy's shoulders.

"What was there?" Daddy asked.

"A bird—only a bird." Daddy let out his breath.

"If you heard a noise in the house you should have taken Orla and gone out, right out."

"Where would I go?" Mammy said, laughing a bit.

"It is no joke," Daddy said, "you should have gone next door, or to any house, to ring the police. You must be careful, Anne."

"I never think of these things," Mammy said and Orla said, "It was only a bird, a little small bird," cupping her hands to show the size. But Daddy was hugging Mammy, even though she had plates in her hand.

The Story of Bran

The Story of Bran

ran was born in the country before Orla was born in Belfast. His mother was called Bessie. His grandmother was called Tudor. When the O'Neills got the fat black pup they called him Bran. That made a change.

Mammy said he was always a polite dog. When he wanted to come in he knocked on the back door with his paw. At the open door he waited until he was told "Come in Bran." He wanted to be a good dog, just as Orla wanted to be a good girl. It was not always easy.

When he was brought up the hills for a walk he arrived above the zoo. The smell of the wild animals made the hair on his neck stand up, and he growled. He would have rushed down to fight them all. Mr. O'Neill had to hold him by his collar. He often felt like fighting other dogs, too, but he learned that nobody likes dog fights. Orla was frightened by them.

Art and Hugh were able to take him for short walks near his house while he was a pup. When he was fully grown he needed long walks. Mr. O'Neill took him up the Cave Hill so that the heather made him clean and shining. He could run in the wind. Then there was old Mr O'Neill who called for him. He was Orla's grandfather.

Sometimes he asked Orla to go for a walk with Bran and himself but Mammy did not let her go very often. She said it was hard for grandparents to mind small children. He had a walking-stick in his right hand, and he held his left hand up behind his back. He often forgot to talk to Orla.

He talked to boys he met on the road because he used to teach boys. One day a boy pointed to a mark across Bran's nose, between his eyes.

"Did he get caught in a mouse trap?" the boy asked.

Bran was ashamed because a cat gave him that mark. He had chased the cat, barking, but it had turned at the corner of his garden, stopped, and lashed out at him with its claws. Orla's Mammy had to clean it and put Dettol on it.

"Did he get caught in a mouse-trap?" the boy asked and Grandad said "Not at all. That's the mark of his glasses." He said it without a smile.

"Does he wear glasses?" the boy asked.

"Only for reading," Grandad said. Orla was delighted but she did not laugh until they were out of sight of the boy.

"What are you laughing at?" Grandad said, taking hold of her hand. "Did you never see his glasses? I suppose he takes them out after you go to bed."

Orla was always glad to have things to bring into school for the nature table. Grandad was very good at finding these. He knew where shiny yellow celandines grew in early Spring. They were down beside a little river and Bran could walk in the water and take a drink. He loved water because he was that kind of dog. Near Easter when they stopped at the side of the road to pick a few primroses, Bran stood well in as he had been taught. He watched that Orla did not step back without thinking. He knew to be afraid of traffic.

At bluebell time they went to the Castle Grounds where there were shoals of bluebells in the woods. They did not pick too many. Grandad showed Orla how to break them half-way down the stalk instead of pulling the big long white parts that grew into the ground. They saw boys and girls with armfuls but that might make the bluebells die out. Bran had a great time dashing in and out among the trees. He could smell rabbits.

In the Summer Orla pulled ferns that she and Art called paint bushes. Grandad said the right name was "horse-tail ferns" and Orla felt very clever saying that in school. Bilberries grew on little short plants on the Cave Hill in the school holidays. Art and Hugh put handfuls of the berries into their mouths. Their tongues and lips were purple. They were good to eat only as soon as they were picked. Mammy made a little tart, once, of bilberries but she said it tasted like sweet soot.

Art asked his grandfather to take him to look for chestnuts in the Autumn. Orla and Bran helped Art to find them among the fallen leaves. Hugh said chestnuts were silly. Orla thought they were beautiful, so brown and glossy when they were fresh. But Art bored a hole through with a steel knitting-needle, and put in a knotted string so that he could play "cheesers" with his friends at school. They then would tire of that game and Mammy would find a shoe-box under his bed half full of dull dried nuts. When Art was told to put them in the bin he planted some and a tree grew. Art was very proud of it. He called it his tree. But Daddy said it would grow far too big.

Bran was a very good dog. Now and again, though, he went off on his own adventures and did not come home for days. Mammy said, "Bran is gone again," and Orla was sad and Mammy was sad. A gloom came down on the house. He came back tired and dusty. One time he lay down on the footpath not far from his own house. A kind woman, who did not know him, got an animal ambulance to put him in the dogs' home. He was very upset. He hurled himself against his cage door all day long. The O'Neills feared a car had run over him. At last Orla's Daddy thought he would check the dogs' home.

"You are a bad dog," Orla said when he was brought home. She was hugging him and crying over him.

But Daddy said "No, he is not. You have seen in your story books, Orla, about a prince who had to ride off on his horse to find a beautiful princess. The prince had to face dangers—monsters and giants and wicked kings. He can't just turn round and ride home. Well, Bran is like that. When he is on his adventures, dogs fight with him and people chase him and throw water round him. It's a dog's life."

"We are all glad you came home at last," Orla said. "It's just as well he did not bring a princess back with him. She would have to share my room." Art and Hugh went off laughing.

Bran was happier before Teddy came. Teddy was a lovely pup and Bran did not like to hear the O'Neills say how nice he looked. Bran's heart twisted when they laughed at the funny puppy things that Teddy did. Orla's Daddy put Teddy into Bran's kennel and told Bran to keep him warm in there. Bran came out of the kennel and slept on the coal. In the morning he was dirty and cross. Hugh said "This is not fair. Bran has a right to his own kennel."

Mammy agreed but they did not know what to do. She said it might have been wiser for Daddy not to bring home a pup. Daddy said what could he do when the man gave it to him.

That night Teddy went into the kennel and Bran stood beside it, his head hanging in misery. He had been out for his walk and he wanted to sleep but he was not going to sleep beside the new pup. Then Mammy said, "Bran, you are my old friend. I'll let you sleep in the kitchen. You are a very sensible, well-trained dog. You can stay here in front of the fire."

Bran came in, wagging his tail a little bit. He was not quite sure what they meant him to do.

"There you are now, Bran. Lie down. That's a good dog. If you want out during the night, just bang the back door. Conn will hear you and come down to look after you." She clapped Daddy on the back and they both laughed. In the morning, Bran was lying on the sofa and that was where he slept from then on.

They tried to train Teddy to eat from his own dish but he came over to Bran's, wagging his whole body, the way pups do. Bran was patient, but he would not touch his food if Teddy had been at it. The whole family told Teddy to leave Bran's dish alone. At last, Bran gave one heartfelt growl. Teddy jumped back, never to touch it again.

He was a nervous dog. He was afraid when other dogs came up to sniff at him. Bran had to chase them away. He was afraid of children on bicycles on the footpath. He dashed away from them into the road. Bran thought he had to look after Teddy.

He knew his job was to look after all the O'Neill family. He had to watch all the people who came to the door. He barked if he did not like the way they looked. He chased cats because they killed birds. He once thought he was chasing a rat but he stopped short when he found it was a hedgehog with its spines out. It had come to live under the hedge. It came out to drink milk. It had a pointed face, a solid body and thin legs like an old, old woman in black stockings. Bran left it alone. When Mrs O'Neill said, "Oh, Bran. A mouse!" he rushed in barking, and hunted. He never caught one. Once when waltz music was playing on the radio Hugh shouted "Strauss." Bran thought he'd said "mouse" and jumped barking to find it. They all laughed at him. He hung his head until Orla hugged him.

One night he was a hero. Mr O'Neill's car was parked outside the gate. Their house was an old house with no garage. They were always going to build one but it was never done. So Mr O'Neill put on locks and alarms at night and went to sleep. Bran slept with one ear awake. Boys steal cars in Belfast. Boys steal cars in Dublin. Mr Kenny, next door, had his car stolen. It was found crashed the next day. So Bran listened every night.

First of all he heard big boys' voices outside the gate. They were standing there. They did not pass by. Bran got off his sofa. He heard them at the car door. He barked—one bark. They were still there. He could hear the rattle of keys. He set up a tirade of barking and banged at the door with his paw. Hugh ran down in his pyjamas and opened the front door. Bran ran out. The boys had the car door open and they had pushed the car a bit down the road. They ran away when Bran rushed out but he chased them until one dropped a big ring of keys.

He lifted that in his mouth and trotted back to his own house. The lights were on in every room. The family stood in the open door waiting to pat him and tell him what a good dog he was. Mrs O'Neill was there and Hugh, Art and Orla. Mr O'Neill was still upstairs putting on his trousers. Teddy was sleeping in his kennel in the yard.

They phoned the police. They were pleased to get all the car keys. That would prevent those boys stealing cars for a little while.

"He is a good dog, that. And well trained," the policeman said. "You should be proud of him." Bran went back to his sofa and fell asleep but his tail wagged all by itself during his dreams.

The Spider

The Spider

**I** think I'll try again to do my knitting," Orla said. It was past the end of the Christmas holidays but the school was still shut because a great many children had flu. Orla never had flu. She did not go out to play because it was cold and wet. There was snow on the hills. She wished she was back in school. Hugh was back at his school. Art was at a jig-saw puzzle on the dining-room table but he would not let Orla help.

"Later on I will," he said "But I want to do some of it myself. It is my puzzle. It was my Christmas present."

"Mammy will you cast on the stitches? Please, Mammy," Orla said. "This time I will knit my duck."

"Lord, love a duck," Daddy said and nobody laughed because he said it every time Orla tried to knit her duck. Orla brought out her short red knitting needles and a ball of yellow wool.

"This wool has lost its nice new look," Mammy said. "Try not to rip it out again."

Orla sat on the edge of a chair, with her back bent and her teeth clenched. She began to knit. "In, round, through, off," she muttered to herself, frowning, at every stitch. Before Christmas, other girls had knitted bright yellow squares. The teacher brought the squares home after school, and the next morning she brought in a bright yellow duck. She sewed up the squares and stuck on brown feet and eyes and a bill. She tied a ribbon round the neck. But Orla was still trying to knit her square. She dropped stitches. She picked up stitches. The stitches stuck on the needles and would not move because they were so tight. She ripped them out, over and over again. Girls who could not read, could knit. Girls who could not write could knit. Girls who were no good at sums could knit. But Orla could not knit.

This time she knew it was no better. She dropped a stitch and Mammy lifted it for her. Her hands grew hot and sticky. She began to cry. Tears scooted out of her eyes and made her wool wet. Bran came and put his head on her knee to comfort her. The tears dropped on his black head. Mammy hugged her.

"Oh, Orla, love. It's not worth crying over."

"But I can't knit," Orla wailed. "The teacher will think I am stupid."

"No, she won't," Mammy said. "She knows you are a clever girl and a good girl."

"Would you not do it for her, Anne?" Daddy said to Mammy.

"No that would be no good," Mammy said. "Art did a lovely square for her but she ripped it out. Anyway, she would never learn that way." She wiped away all the tears and kissed the top of Orla's head. "I tell you what," she said. "I'll put a hot water bottle in your bed and you can have a rest. I'll call you before tea. After tea I'll sit down beside you and keep an eye on it stitch by stitch. We'll throw away all the scruffy wool and make a fresh start."

Orla had a hot water bottle the shape of a brown bear. She hugged it in bed. The sky was grey outside. It was not dark so Mammy did not turn on the light.

A spider had made a web above the light. It spun itself a thread and dangled down to look at Orla. It watched her for a long time. Then it asked,

"What is the matter? I often see you all smiles. What is wrong?"

"I can't knit," Orla said and she nearly cried again.

"It's the way you sit," the spider said. "I've seen you hunched up. You must sit right to knit right. I know. I make beautiful webs. Do you admire my beautiful webs?"

"My Mammy will wipe down all your webs," Orla said because she was still cross.

"Stupid people! Stupid people!" the spider said, now cross too. "Always wiping down my beautiful webs."

"My Mammy is not stupid," Orla said.

"Not as stupid as the woman next door. She wipes them off the hedge in Autumn. Beautiful webs, sparkling with dew and out she comes and wipes them off," the spider said.

"Spiders have no brains," Orla said

"Spiders have brains," the spider was indignant. "I read a book—"

"You could not read a book," Orla said.

"I can read books," the spider insisted. "When I see books open I read them. I do not stay too long for fear stupid people would shut them on me. You think only your Bran can read."

"I suppose you need glasses too," Orla scoffed.

"I do not need glasses. I see very well. I have eight eyes. I don't know how I would wear all the glasses," the spider laughed. Orla was surprised to hear the laugh and she smiled too.

"Eight eyes," she said turning to see them.

"I am telling you about the book," the spider went on.

"It was your Daddy's book. He left it open on the floor beside his chair. It said my brain evolved. Did your brain evolve?" the spider asked.

"I don't know," Orla said. "My brain was in my head when I was born."

"You ask your Daddy about that word in his book," the spider told her. "There it was written down that the spider's brain evolved around the tube she eats through. I can take only liquids because the tube is so narrow. If it grew any wider I would not have enough brains to find food. If my brain grew any bigger I would not be able to swallow anything. Isn't that a fine puzzle for me. You think your knitting is a problem."

"It is too," Orla said, upset again.

"Here is a riddle for you," the spider laughed. "Why did the fly fly?"

Orla thought for a little while and then gave up.

"Because the spider spied her," the spider laughed again. "Isn't that a good riddle? Do you get it?"

It took Orla a minute to work it out. "You eat flies," she accused the spider.

"Your grandfather says it is a very healthy thing to have spiders around the house," the spider said. "He knows it is good to clear away flies. He is a sensible man."

"Some people are afraid of you," Orla said, because she had met such people.

"It is very odd indeed," the spider said, shaking her head so that her thread waved to and fro.

"How about Little Miss Muffet?" Orla asked. "She ran away from you, didn't she?

"Poor little Miss Muffet," the spider smiled. "It was her father's fault. He thought spiders were great. He had crowds of us in the house. Dr. Muffet, he was called, and he made medicine out of spiders. He wanted her to drink it when she was sick. She ran away from the medicine. I am very glad she did. There would have been no spiders left if people thought they were good to take as medicine." Orla thought of all the people with flu having to eat squashed spiders, and she giggled. The spider laughed too but, "It's not such a good joke for us," she said. "You never know the day somebody will try it again and wipe us out. We've been in the world for millions of years, you know, far longer than people."

"I am still thinking of my knitting," Orla said.

"It's an odd thing," the spider said. "As soon as my little spiderlings grow big enough to make webs they will know how. They will not begin until the days are a bit warmer, but I will not have to teach them. They will know all the right ways, all the patterns."

"It is well for them," Orla sighed.

"Maybe it is because we have been around for millions of years. Maybe in millions of years, wee girls will know how to knit when they are six years old, without being taught." The spider put one of her eight feet to hold up her chin, thinking.

"This is no good to me," Orla said.

"Listen," the spider said. "I have told you it's the way you sit. Sit up straight and take a deep breath or two, and think of something nice. Your Mammy will see that it works. Oh, I hear her on the stairs. Don't forget to tell your Daddy the riddle. I'll speel away up to my little spiderlings. See you."

Orla's Mammy opened the door and turned on the light. There was no sign of the spider.

"Did you have a good sleep?" Mammy said.

"No, of course not," Orla said. "It is not night-time."

"You should have put on your lamp then," Mammy said. "You were lying in the dark."

"Was I?" Orla asked, because it had not seemed like that. She had seen the spider clearly.

"Hurry up, love," Mammy said as Orla sat on the floor to put on her shoes. "I've made French toast just for your tea and I want you to eat it while it is hot."

When she had eaten up all her French toast and drunk her milk, Orla asked, "Daddy why did the fly fly?"

"Because it had to hurry for its tea," Daddy said and Orla laughed and shook her head.

"Because its shoes were being mended in the shoemaker's," he said and she shouted, "No. Do you give up?"

"Indeed, I do not," Daddy said. "Let me think. Because the sea was too stormy to go by boat."

"Oh give up," Hugh said. "You are not a bit funny."

But Orla was laughing. "It's because the spider spied her," she told him and he said it over twice before he said, "Oh yes. That's a good one."

"It's a very old one," Hugh said. "I heard it years ago."

He had been happy with Art at his jig-saw but now he knew it was time to go and do his homework.

"Maybe," Daddy said, "if the spiders had not chased the flies they would not have grown wings. We'll never know."

"What does evolve mean?" Orla remembered she was to ask. "Is it about something like that?"

Daddy looked at Mammy and asked "Where did we get such a clever wee girl?"

So Orla was smiling when she began to knit. She watched Mammy cast on the stitches. She was not expected to do that herself. When she took over the needles, she said "I am to sit up straight with my two feet on the floor."

"Oh yes," Mammy said. "You were told that in school, of course. And remember the three deep breaths the teacher told you to take." Orla did not say a word about the spider but she smiled to herself and she knit the first row easily. Mammy counted the stitches to make sure none had crept in or out. Orla did the next row.

After a few rows she began to hum a tune to herself because she was sure now that she could knit. In a short time Mammy cast off the stitches and there the square was, complete.

Orla smoothed it over her knee.

"I'll press it under a damp cloth with the iron," Mammy said, "to make sure it turns into a beautiful duck."

"It's not every day a girl learns how to knit a duck," Daddy said.

"Just as well," Mammy said. Orla laughed because she felt the same way.

"I'll help Art with his jig-saw now, if he lets me," she said. Straight away she found three pieces and pressed them into place.

"That's great," Art said. "I was looking for those for ages."

Orla was a happy girl.

Children's
POOLBEG

Orla Was Six
   Mary Beckett   £2.99
Candy on the Dart
   Ita Daly   £2.99
When the Luvenders
  Came to Merrick Town
   June Considine   £3.50
Discoveries
   Clodagh Corcoran ed £4.99
Baker's Dozen
   Clodagh Corcoran ed £3.50
Children's Quiz Book No. 1
   Robert Duffy   £2.99
Children's Quiz Book No. 2
   Robert Duffy   £2.99
Joe in the Middle
   Tony Hickey   £2.99
Where is Joe?
   Tony Hickey   £3.50
Spike and the Professor
   Tony Hickey   £2.99
Blanketland
   Tony Hickey   £2.99
The Bridge of Feathers
   Eamon Kelly   £2.99
The Turf-Cutter's Donkey
   Patricia Lynch   £2.99
Brogeen Follows the
  Magic Tune
   Patricia Lynch   £2.99

Brogeen and the Green
  Shoes
   Patricia Lynch   £3.50
Patsy-O
   Bryan MacMahon   £2.99
Growing Things
   Sean McCann   £2.99
Shoes and Ships and
  Sealing-Wax
   A Book of Quotations for Children
   Sean McMahon ed   £2.99
The Poolbeg Book of
  Children's Verse
   Sean McMahon ed   £4.95
The Viking Princess
   Michael Mullen   £2.99
The Little Drummer Boy
   Michael Mullen   £2.99
The Little Black Hen
   Eileen O'Faoláin   £2.99
An Nollaig Thiar
   Breandán Ó hEithir £2.99
Bugsy Goes to Limerick
   Carolyn Swift   £2.99
Robbers on TV
   Carolyn Swift   £2.99
A Little Man in England
   Shaun Traynor   £2.99
Hugo O'Huge
   Shaun Traynor   £2.99

The Turf Cutter's Donkey

and

Brogeen Follows the Magic Tune

by

Patricia Lynch

"Classics of Irish Children's Literature"

Irish Independent

£2.99